POCKET · PUFFINS

D1059597

Puffin Books, Penguin Books Ltd, Harmondsworth, Middlesex, England
Viking Penguin Inc., 40 West 23rd Street, New York, New York 10010, U.S.A.
Penguin Books Australia Ltd, Ringwood, Victoria, Australia
Penguin Books Canada Ltd, 2801 John Street, Markham, Ontario, Canada L3R 1B4
Penguin Books (N.Z.) Ltd, 182-190 Wairau Road, Auckland 10, New Zealand

First published by Ernest Benn Ltd 1981
First published 1987 in Pocket Puffins
by Puffin Books in association with Moonlight Publishing Ltd
Copyright © Colin McNaughton, 1981

Made and printed in Italy by La Editoriale Libraria

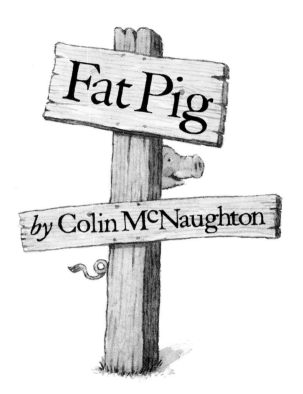

Fat Pig

by Colin McNaughton

One morning, Fat Pig was taking a
walk around the farmyard.

"Morning Granny Hen."
"Morning Shaughn Sheep."
"Morning Byron Turkey."
And so on; all was well on the farm.
Or so it seemed.

As Fat Pig passed the farm house window, he heard Farmer Pyjama's deep voice and it made his marrow bone jelly quiver. He went back to his sty and cried so loudly that all the other animals came to see what was the matter.

"What's wrong?" clucked Granny Hen.

"It's Farmer Pyjama," sobbed Fat Pig. "He said that in two weeks time I shall be just the, *sniff,* right size."

"The right size for what?" asked Granny Hen.

"Pork, *sniff,* chops and bacon. Whatever can I, *sniff,* do?"

"You'll just have to diet," baahed Shaughn Sheep, who wasn't as daft as he looked.

"Dye what?" asked Fat Pig.

"Diet, you fool, not dye-it. You must lose weight," shouted his friends. "We'll help you."

Fat Pig was so happy he danced a jig.

That evening, the animals worked out a plan to save Fat Pig's bacon.

But now, Fat Pig was not so pleased. Up at the crack of dawn for exercises and just one miserable bowl of pigswill to eat.

"It's for your own good," said Byron.

"Odd," muttered Fat Pig, as he was getting ready for bed, "but whenever someone says, 'It's for your own good,' it's always something nasty."

"OCH THE NOODLE NOO,"
yodelled Brewster MacRooster, the
farm cock.

Fat Pig half-opened one bleary eye,
turned over and went back to sleep.

"Get up, you lazy pig," crowed
Brewster, "say 'Good Morning' to the
sun."

"Morning," grunted Fat Pig
miserably.

Jack Daw brought him a small
bowl.

"But . . ." started Fat Pig.

"No buts," said Granny Hen.

One-and-a-half mouthfuls later, Fat
Pig had finished his breakfast.

"Now," said Granny Hen. "Off
you go on a ten-mile run. Jack Daw
will show you the way."

So, tired and hungry, Fat Pig set
out.

After two minutes he had a stitch in his right side.

After three minutes he had a stitch in his left side.

After four minutes he collapsed in a heap on the ground.

"PORK CHOPS," screeched Jack Daw.

Fat Pig sprang to his feet and ran like the wind; or at least, like a stiff breeze.

Every time he slowed down, Jack Daw would scream, ''BACON'' or ''BUTCHER'' or ''PIG'S TROTTERS.''

Fat Pig staggered back into the farmyard; but there was more to come.

The rest of the day was a nightmare; steam baths, exercises and . . . swimming.

"SWIMMING," protested Fat Pig. "Pigs can't swim."

"Well, it's time they learned," said Ronald Duck.

As he lay in his sty that night, Fat Pig had an idea.

In the morning, he said, "I think I'll go on a long run today. Much the best way to lose weight. Don't bother to come with me, Jack, I can find my own way." And off he went, leaving behind some very puzzled and suspicious faces.

For the next few days Fat Pig went running. But he didn't seem to be getting any thinner.

"It's muscles," he said, with a guilty look.

"Muscles, my foot," said Byron. "Are you sure you haven't been eating on the sly?"

"What? Me?" stuttered Fat Pig. "I'm out running all day."

When Fat Pig was asleep everyone gathered in the barn. They agreed that next day Jack Daw should follow Fat Pig, because, as Brewster

remarked, "There's something fishy about that pig."

Next day, when Fat Pig trotted out towards Four Acre Wood, Jack Daw was close behind him.

It was not long before he found the secret of Fat Pig's grow-larger diet.

While Fat Pig tucked into a huge trough of pigswill, his two cousins, Tusk and Snorter Wilde-Pigge, stood smirking behind him.

"You'll soon be so fat that Farmer
Pyjama will enter you in the Pig of the
Year Show. You're bound to win First
Prize," they said.

"But Granny Hen said . . ."
slobbered Fat Pig.

"Who cares about what the stupid old hen says?" said Tusk and Snorter, and they danced round Fat Pig, chanting a silly song.

When in doubt
Stuff your snout
With pigswill, oats and hay.
Eat your fill
And forget the bill
Farmer Pyjama will pay, will pay
Farmer Pyjama will pay.

Jack hurried back. When the other animals heard what had happened there were shouts of "Ungrateful Pig," "Cheat" and other things, much worse.

"Listen," shouted Sam Crow above the noise. "It's no good blaming Fat Pig. You all know what he's like when there's food around. It's those twins, Tusk and Snorter. But we haven't a moment to lose. Tomorrow's the day

that Farmer Pyjama is going to weigh
Fat Pig and we must find a way to
save him.''

   They all tried to think of an idea.
Then suddenly, Brewster MacRooster
crowed, ''I've got the answer! But I
don't think that Fat Pig will like it one
little bit.''
   All the animals met outside Fat
Pig's sty the next morning.

"Och the Noodle Noooooo,"
yodelled Brewster.

"Grunt," said Fat Pig and tried to
go back to sleep. In his dream he had
just won the Pig of the Year prize and
crowds of animals were shouting his
name; but the strange thing was that
when he opened his eyes they were
still shouting.

"FAT PIG, FAT PIG, RUN FOR
YOUR LIFE! THE BUTCHER IS
HERE. PORK CHOPS, BACON,
SAUSAGES."

Fat Pig was terrified. He jumped to
his feet and ran as he had never run
before.

"RUN, RUN, HE'S BEHIND
YOU!" shouted the voices.

And Fat Pig ran. Above him, Jack
Daw and Sam Crow screeched,
"FASTER, FASTER, HE'S RIGHT
ON YOUR TAIL!"

Out of the corner of his eye, Fat Pig
could see a big butcher's knife
swishing back and forth and flashing
in the sun.

On and on he ran. Up hills and down valleys. Into woods, across meadows. Jumping fences and scampering over bridges, until he found himself back in the farmyard again. He could go no further.

"All right," Fat Pig gasped.
"You've, *snort and gasp,* got me!" He
raised his head and saw Farmer
Pyjama standing over him.

"Dear me," said the farmer.
"What's going on here? Who is this
skinny pig with a butcher's knife tied
to his tail? Bless my soul, it's Fat Pig!
And he's as thin as a rake. He can't
go to market like that!" And Farmer
Pyjama stamped back to the
farmhouse muttering to himself.

The other animals then told Fat Pig about the trick they had played. At first he was very angry, but he soon realised that they had saved his life.

"What a fool I was to listen to Tusk and Snorter," he said.

Sam Crow said that he would fly over to Boar Manor and tell the piglets' father, old Colonel Wilde-Pigge, what had happened. The Colonel was a boar who didn't stand for any nonsense.

Fat Pig promised to stay thin, but no one believed him. And sure enough, as the days passed, he grew fatter and fatter.

Burying his face up to the ears in his trough he could be heard muttering, ''Next market day is an awfully long way off . . .''

COLIN McNAUGHTON was born and brought up near Newcastle upon Tyne in the north of England. He left school at 16 and did all sorts of jobs for a year before ending up at art school in London. His first children's book was published in 1976 when he was still at college. Since then a rich variety of books have poured from his pen, including *The Rat Race, King Nonn the Wiser, Walk Rabbit Walk* (with Elizabeth Attenborough) and the *Red Nose Readers* and *Happy Families* series (with Allan Ahlberg.) Now, as well as books, he has been working on stage productions of *Fat Pig* and has written his first collection of poems.

He lives in London with his wife, Françoise, and their two children, Ben and Timothy.

"The only picture books I knew as a child were the comic annuals I was given at Christmas: Beano, Dandy, Topper, Eagle *and* Lion. *Looking back, it's not difficult to see that these comics were the main influence on my work. These, and the films I saw every Saturday morning at my local cinema. Pirate films, knights in armour, cowboys and Indians. Although today I am married, with two wild sons and a lovely French wife, I still like the same things. I guess I never grew up."*
Colin McNaughton

There are other POCKET PUFFINS for you to enjoy:

Bill and Stanley by Helen Oxenbury
A busy afternoon for Bill and his best friend, Stanley the dog.

Peter and the Wolf by Sergei Prokofiev and Erna Voigt
The well-known musical tale, beautifully illustrated.

Mr Potter's Pigeon by P. Kinmonth and R. Cartwright
The touching story of an old man and his pet racing pigeon, with award-winning pictures.

Panda's Puzzle by Michael Foreman
Panda travels from the Himalayas to the United States to find the answer to a very important question.

Billy Goat and His Well-Fed Friends by N. Hogrogian
Billy Goat doesn't want to end up as the Farmers supper...

This Little Pig-A-Wig by Lenore and Erik Blegvad
A lovely, lively collection of pig-poems old and new.

The Pearl by Helme Heine
Beaver realises that there are greater riches in life than even the loveliest of pearls.

The Feathered Ogre by Lee Lorenz
Little Jack the Piper outwits the ferocious ogre and plucks his golden feathers. A very funny fairy tale.

If I Had... by Mercer Mayer
'If only I had a gorilla, a crocodile, a snake...then no-one would pick on me...' A small boy's daydreams find a real-life solution.